PRIDE & PEDIGREE

SADDLES & SCOUNDRELS

JENNIFER MOORE

CARPE VITAM
PRESS LLC

For Angela Woiwode, lover of dogs and words.

CHAPTER 1

*A*lastair Charles Rutherford III stared into the mirror, concentrating as he tied his ascot. Renn, his valet had taught him a rather complicated knot, and Alastair was determined to master it. He twisted and pulled the silk into place with care, and once he deemed it finished, he studied it in the mirror, pleased with the result.

Renn brought his waistcoat, brushing it as he walked. When he came near, he peered at the ascot. "A fine attempt, sir."

Alastair sighed, pulling apart his failed attempt and lifting his chin to allow his valet to have a go.

Renn fashioned the knot with quick fingers. He stepped back and looked it over with a critical eye, then gave a satisfied nod.

Alastair regarded the ascot in the mirror. Renn's work was exceptional. He lifted his brow, meeting the valet's steady gaze, and he tipped his head in acquiescence. Renn's lips pulled so slightly that if he hadn't known the man for the entirety of his twenty-eight years, Alastair wouldn't have noticed it. This scant change in expression was the equivalent of an enormous and very cheeky grin.

Alastair slid his arms into his coat, and upon receiving the valet's approval on his presentation, he proceeded down the staircase into the entry hall and nodded to the footman who pulled open the grand doors. When he stepped outside, the scents of the garden roses and the wisteria mingled together agreeably. He paused and inhaled. Failure to appreciate the flowers would be a slight to his mother's memory.

Alastair was immensely pleased to have returned to his family home after the inconvenience of relocating for nine months while the ancient plumbing was updated to modern standards. The garden's full blooms were an especially welcoming sight after such a long absence.

He continued down the stone steps to his waiting carriage. The evening was just starting to darken and the air was warm. There were only a few clouds, and the moon would be full. A perfect night for Mrs. Mumford's garden reception. And he had it on good authority that Miss Annalise Brittany would be in attendance this evening. He had developed an acquaintance with the young woman, and found her sufficiently agreeable. According to his solicitor, Miss Brittany's family was well connected, and her fortune substantial. Precisely the criteria his father had specified in his dying wishes. A woman of excellent social and financial standing.

Alastair nodded to the coachman and put his foot on the mounting step, but hearing his name called, he paused before pulling himself up.

"Mr. Rutherford, sir!" Cecil Babbage, the kennel master was running toward him. "Wait, if you please!"

Alastair stepped down, feeling apprehensive. Cecil would only come for him directly if there was an emergency. A dog must be ill or injured or...worse. "What is it, Mr. Babbage?"

"Lulabelle." The kennel master was breathless.

Alastair's stomach sank. He strode quickly toward the kennels, nearly breaking into a run. It couldn't be Lulabelle. Not only was she one of—if not *the*—most valuable breeding fox terrier dams in the country, she was the last of the litter his father had bred before his death. And with her playful nature and deep brown eyes, she was Alastair's favorite.

Cecil rushed up behind him. "No, sir. Lulabelle isn't there."

Alastair stopped, whirling around.

"She's managed to open the gate to her pen, sir. I've looked everywhere, but..."

Alastair continued to the dog yard, past the whelping shed and to Lulabelle's enclosure. He looked at the latch, seeing right away how she'd managed to release it. She must have jumped up and pulled down on the latch with her paw. He shook his head, "Too intelligent for her own good."

"I'm sorry, sir. I—"

"Where have you searched, Mr. Babbage?" Alastair cut him off. Time was of the essence. The longer they dallied, the farther away Lulabelle would be.

"Down in the dingle, sir. And in the meadow east of the house. All the places I take the hounds for exercise and training. I couldn't go farther abroad. Not on foot. The lads and I have looked for hours. But we've seen no sign o' her."

Where else would she go? Alastair tapped his chin as worry spread cold over his skin. She had been a small puppy when the plumbing work began and had spent most of her life at the household's temporary residence on the far side of town. Her lacking familiarity with this property meant the little dog could easily become lost on the manor grounds and the woods beyond.

"Return to the woods," he told Cecil. "I'll—" A thought struck him, and he stopped, mid-sentence.

He recalled tales of dogs making their way over long distances to return to familiar places and realized he might have underestimated her navigation instincts. Had Lulabelle escaped in an attempt to find her old home? With darkness falling, Alastair made the decision in an instant, calling for the groom as he hurried toward the stable.

As his horse was being saddled, he sent the carriage on to Mrs. Mumford's with his apologies. He would join the party late, if he was able. He shook off the worry that another suitor might capture Miss Brittney's affections. Finding his dam was of the utmost importance, though it was a pity Renn's handiwork with an ascot would go unadmired.

A moment later, he was astride his horse and galloping along the road toward Freshford. Though the route through the town was not the shortest, Alastair considered it safer for the horse in the dark. He rode along the High Street, slowing only to keep his mount from slipping on the paving stones, and once he was through, he spurred the animal on toward the property that had been his temporary home. The three-mile ride took half an hour, and the entire time, his mind spun with worries for his dog.

Nearing the gates leading to the property, Alastair slowed. He saw no sign of Lulabelle, and doubt started to itch at him. He had been so certain she had returned here, but what if he had acted too quickly? Was he wasting valuable time on a far-fetched hunch? Perhaps he should have remained and searched near the manor house.

He pushed the thoughts away, resolving to trust his instinct and squinted into the darkness, searching for movement. Moonlight gave the scene a silver and purple hue. "Lulabelle!" he called. He dismounted, tied the horse to a gate post and continued on foot. The house, as far as he knew was empty, and so he headed in the opposite direction, coming to the barn where the temporary kennels had been. Perhaps the dog had thought to return to her former enclosure. He pushed open the door, calling inside. But Lulabelle wasn't there.

A hill at the back of the property led down to the river, one of Lulabelle's favorite places to play. Alastair stepped as quickly as he dared in the darkness, calling as he went. The air cooled as he drew near to the water. The river was deeper than it had been in early spring, filling him with unease. He turned downstream, following the dark ribbon of water calling for Lulabelle as he went. The land rose up on the far side of the river, making a narrow sort of valley that occasionally led through clusters of trees and thickets. Here and there, a stone bridge crossed to the other side.

Occasionally, Alastair stepped too close to the water, and his foot stuck in the thick mud. Once, he nearly lost his boot, and he winced, knowing the muck must be damaging the fine leather.

After an hour, the ground became level, and the river split into smaller streams as it flowed through meadows and farmland. Alastair scanned his eyes over the vista, searching for a sign of movement.

Seeing none, he retraced his steps, deciding to search upstream. But when he came near the house, he saw a light glowing in a rear window. It must be occupied after all. Perhaps the inhabitants had seen Lulabelle, or they might be persuaded to join in the search.

Alastair started up the hill, but hearing a deep growl, he halted. A large shape moved in the shadows ahead, a beast on four legs.

He looked around for a stick or something to defend himself as his mind fumbled to recognize what the shape could be. A bear? A wolf? There were neither in England. And he'd never heard a fox make such a sound.

A banging noise startled him.

The growling came again, and Alastair squinted, trying to make out the source of the sounds. His mouth was dry, and thoughts of supernatural creatures made their way into his mind, which he knew was nonsense. Nevertheless…

"Away with you!" a woman called. Alastair felt a measure of relief at the human-ness of the voice. The banging came again. It sounded as if a heavy object were being hit against metal.

The source of the noise, and the voice, stepped into a ray of moonlight, and Alastair could make out the silhouette of a woman carrying a pot and a ladle. She was slender and tall, her hair unbound and hanging in waves over her shoulders. The shadow, still too large to be identified, joined her.

"You have no business here," the woman's loud voice seemed much less ominous now that Alastair knew its source. "Go now! Or I shall command him to attack."

Alastair must look a fool lurking about in the dark in his festive finery, now muddied and snagged. He held up his hands to show he held no weapon and made his voice as non-threatening as possible. "If you please, madam. I am merely looking for my dog."

"What dog?" Her posture didn't relax, but her voice seemed to be a bit less accusatory.

"She is a fox terrier, white with tan markings on her face and ears. A black saddle. Fourteen inches at the withers and weighs just over one stone. She wears a leather collar with my initials. ACR." The woman didn't move, so he continued, feeling as if an explanation was required. "You see, I used to live here." He motioned to the house behind her. "And I thought—"

At his movement, the animal growled again.

Alastair froze.

"It is all right, Major," the woman said in a low voice. She turned back toward the house. "Come along, sir. Your animal is inside."

A wave of relief washed over him, and Alastair hurried to follow the woman, and what he could now see was an enormous dog, toward the rear door of the house.

He reached to open the door for her, but the woman pushed through. The dog followed.

Alastair stepped into the kitchen, a room he'd rarely entered when he'd occupied this house. He glanced around, seeing water on the stone floor. Muddy towels and a wet apron were hanging over a wash basin.

The woman engaged the gaslights, giving Alastair his first full view of her. She was young, likely twenty or perhaps slightly older. And, as he'd seen, tall—he estimated only a few inches shy of his own height of six feet—and slender. Her skin was tanned, as if she'd spent time outdoors, and her hair was a light brown. Not a traditional beauty, but there was something about her that was very intriguing to look at.

She set the pot she'd been banging onto the table, but kept hold of the wooden ladle and studied him in return, her gray eyes appearing to calculate his character.

Under her scrutiny, Alastair stood taller, although he immediately felt foolish for the action. What did this woman's opinion of him matter?

In the light, Alastair could finally see the beast—*Major*—beside her. The dog was enormous. Over thirty inches at the withers, and it must weigh 250 pounds. He tried to discern the various breeds from which it obtained its characteristics. A mastiff surely gave the beast its size. Its hair was long and thick, which he assumed was the contribution of a setter or a collie. And the floppy ears and multi-colored fur were possibly from...a beagle? In all, the creature was the ugliest mongrel he'd ever beheld, and it was impossible to believe this woman allowed it in the house.

The young lady folded her arms, still holding the ladle. "Major found your dog, cold and muddy down at the river," she said.

From her tone, he understood he was to be grateful. But if she thought he was about to thank a dog, she was sorely mistaken.

She patted Major on his head. "Good dog," she said. "Off you go, now."

The animal obediently padded from the room on feet the size of pies.

"Thank you," Alastair said, now that it was clear to whom the sentiment was directed. "And I apologize, we have not been properly introduced." He meant to follow the rules of polite behavior, even if this woman did not. "Alastair Rutherford." He inclined his head.

She gave no recognition at his name, which he found surprising. But, as she was newly occupying this house, perhaps she'd come from outside the county.

"Nora Winters," she offered, glancing down at his muddy boots. "You are finely dressed for an excursion to the river."

"I was on my way to a party when I discovered Lulabelle was missing."

"Lulabelle." She spoke the name as if she were sampling it, but her expression gave no indication of her assessment. "Come along, Mr. Rutherford. Lulabelle is in the parlour." Miss Winters motioned with the ladle and started down the corridor.

Moving with careful steps, Alastair followed. He'd considered removing his boots, but the thought of walking around this house in stockinged feet was so undignified that he could not bring himself to do it.

At the doorway to the parlour, she stopped, turning to him, and holding up a finger in front of her mouth, directing him to be silent.

He entered the room behind her, seeing the familiar furniture, still arranged in the same manner, but with some subtle differences. Trinkets on the shelves, a pile of books on a table, an extra lamp. The room appeared *cozier*, as if it were not only used for visitors, but as a living space. One book was open and overturned on chair. A soft blanket lay over the chair's arm, as if Miss Winters had been inter-rupted—most likely by the dogs. The sight made Alastair curious to know what she had been reading. But he cast off the thought. What did it matter when he'd not be interacting with her again once he left the house?

His glance moved to the sofa, and to the reason for their silence. An older woman with white curls and forgotten needlework on her lap snored softly, her head resting on her shoulder.

On the rug in front of the sofa, and looking every bit as large as the furniture, Major was curled around a crumpled blanket. And within...

Lulabelle! In his effort to avoid calling out her name and disturbing the old woman's sleep, he forgot his muddy shoes and hurried to his dog.

Major growled as he neared, but stopped at Miss Winters's soft command.

Alastair scooped Lulabelle into his arms. She was still wet, but she was clean. She burrowed into his coat as he held her.

He stood and whispered to Miss Winters, "I am very grateful—"

She shushed him, motioning with a lift of her chin toward the doorway, and the pair returned to the kitchen. Major followed, carrying Lulabelle's blanket in his mouth.

"You should take better care of your dog, sir." Miss Winters took the blanket from Major and placed it over Lulabelle, tucking it around where she shivered in Alastair's arms. "She could become chilled and take a fever."

Alastair did not appreciate the accusation in her tone. "I am very aware of a dog's proper care, Miss Winters. I am rather an expert."

She tipped her head, her gaze going to Lulabelle and then back to his, saying without words that the cold dog in his arms indicated otherwise.

Alastair's ears went hot. "I'll have you know, Lulabelle is one of, if not *the*, most prized dogs of her breed in the kingdom. Her future offspring have already been spoken for, some by Prince Bertie himself." He watched for her reaction, ready to graciously accept her apology.

"She seems to be very valuable, sir. It is no wonder you were so eager to find her."

Her tone held something Alastair couldn't quite identify. Disappointment? Challenge? Though he couldn't understand why, he took offense to it, and his anger rose.

"This dam is very important, and near to breeding age, which is why I must keep her out of the reach of common mongrels." He sniffed at Major, leaving no doubt as to his meaning.

"I beg your pardon, Mr. Rutherford." Miss Winters's voice went cold. "My *mongrel* saved Lulabelle." She pointed with the ladle to each animal in turn. "And, that makes him even more valuable than your precious purebred."

Alastair held back a laugh. "Hardly."

"By your own reasoning, Lulabelle's value comes from the pups she will bear. If Major saved both Lulabelle and her future offspring, then his value is of greater worth."

This rationale was ridiculous. "A dog's value doesn't come from his behavior, but from rarity, breeding and ancestry." He gave a long look toward Major, shaking his head. "Unfortunately, such factors are not attributes for your…"

"Mongrel?" Miss Winters's eyes were hard. She slapped the ladle into the palm of her hand and took a step toward him. "Well, Mr. Rutherford…" She took another step, crowding him toward the door. "In that case, you should leave quickly. Before Lulabelle's reputation is sullied. You know how people talk."

A moment later, the door slammed and Alastair stood on the other side, Lulabelle in his arms. He wrapped the dog tighter in the blanket and started around the house toward where he'd left his horse.

"I'm afraid your rescuer doesn't much care for me," he muttered to the dog. "I'll send a small reward for her role in keeping you safe, but I won't be disappointed to never see Miss Winters again. And I'd be much obliged if you remain in your kennel from now on."

Alastair rode home slowly, one hand holding the reins and the other arm bundling an increasingly squirming Lulabelle. His thoughts returned to what had transpired that night. Who were Miss Winters and the old woman? Where had they come from? And what explained a beastly dog with obviously impeccable training? Miss Winters was certainly a peculiar sort who raised endless questions. Alastair almost regretted that he'd never learn the answers.

CHAPTER 2

*N*ora lifted her basket onto her hip and reached back to take Mrs. Shaw's arm as the older woman stepped down off the stone bridge. "Have a care," she said. "The mud here is thicker than treacle."

Major stood close, as he always did, watching with his deep wise eyes to make certain the women met with no mishap.

"Thank you, my dear." Mrs. Shaw placed her steps carefully, leaning both on Nora and on her walking stick to avoid the mud. Once she was safely away from the bank, she dabbed at her forehead with a handkerchief. "Goodness me, I would look a fool if I'd fallen in, wouldn't I?"

Nora laughed, but the idea wasn't humorous at all. This particular estuary of the River Avon was deep after the rainfall of the past week, and the mud on the banks so thick, a person could easily become stuck as she tried to get out of the water. The very idea gave Nora a tinge of unease, and she watched Mrs. Shaw closely until she was safely on the path above the bank.

The women had walked into Westwood two or three times per week since they'd taken the house outside of town. But this was the first time they'd attempted this particular route, a trail through the woods that was shorter, but not smooth and with a much more precarious bridge. Mrs. Shaw had insisted on the shortcut as they made their way home, but Nora worried it was more of a strain on Mrs. Shaw's strength than she let on. She would have to talk Mrs. Shaw into taking their regular, longer path in the future, but for now, she needed to convince the old woman to stop and recover her breath.

"Shall we rest?" Nora asked. She pointed at a flat patch of earth beneath the shade of a beech tree. "This appears rather a nice place to sit for a spell."

"If I sit down on the ground, it'll be impossible to stand back up." Mrs. Shaw shook her head. "I've no need of a rest. The two of you need to stop mollycoddling me," She waved a finger back and forth between Nora and Major. "It makes me feel old."

Nora settled for setting an extra slow pace and did not point out that at eighty-two years, Mrs. Shaw *was* old. She had been old for as long as Nora had known her. But lately, her limp had become more pronounced and she moved slower. The reminder that her dear companion would not always be here was a painful one. Despite their age difference, the two had been friends since Nora was seven years old, and had been found—as Mrs. Shaw liked to tell the tale—sound asleep atop an open volume of Chaucer in the Shaw's library.

Nora didn't remember the day. Nor could she believe she'd had the audacity to creep into a stranger's house and help herself to the library. She could understand why she'd done it, however. Nora's own home was hardly a place of peace and learning, and with the chaos of nine brothers and sisters and parents who were in turn absent and harried, she had no doubt looked for a quiet place to escape to. And the sanctuary of the Shaw's enormous library with its leather chairs, deep carpets, and floor-to-ceiling bookshelves must have been too much of a temptation.

She linked her arm with Mrs. Shaw's, and they proceeded along the path following the stream toward their house. Major walked ahead, and Nora knew with the dog leading the way, they had nothing to worry about. Major would stop at a rock or a stick in the path if he was worried the women might trip, or warn them of briars or even a low hanging branch, and he'd continue on only when he was certain they had safely avoided the obstacle. And that was to say nothing of any people they might pass. She almost felt sorry for any bandit or highwayman who might think the women easy prey. Not that they had met with any sort of unpleasantness since moving to the country. It seemed as if crime simply did not exist in such a tranquil place as Westwood.

"We're nearly there." Mrs. Shaw pointed with her walking stick toward the top of the roof poking up over the trees ahead. "This route is indeed faster."

"Faster, yes," Nora agreed. "But I do not think I would choose it in the future. Not with—"

Major's bark cut off her words. Nora and Mrs. Shaw both paused, peering ahead, but the dog was out of sight, on the other side of the trees.

"Major?" Nora called.

The dog barked again, but the sound wasn't his usual warning. This was his happy greeting, the same one he gave to her when she arrived home after being away. But Nora couldn't imagine who he could be excited to see, not unless one of their old friends from Bristol had arrived for an unexpected visit.

Nora looked at Mrs. Shaw, and seeing confusion in her friend's expression as well, they quickened their steps to catch up to Major.

When they came around the trees, they saw Major chasing after a smaller dog, then turning and allowing the dog to chase him.

Nora sighed. "Lulabelle."

"Oh, it's the terrier we found a few days ago, isn't it?" Mrs. Shaw squinted to get a better look at the animal. "The special hound that belongs to Mr. Alastair Rutherford of Durham Manor." She spoke the name with exaggerated formality as if she were the Master of Ceremonies making introductions at a royal ball.

"It is," Nora said. "Precious Lulabelle the purebred fox terrier who is more valuable than any other dog in the kingdom." She rolled her eyes. "And I imagine her owner will not be pleased to discover that she's gone again—and associating with such riffraff."

13

After hearing of Nora's interaction with the man, Mrs. Shaw had made inquiries about him in town. They had learned that, not only was he descended from a long line of acclaimed dog breeders, but he was also wealthy. Extremely so, which made him—according to both Mrs. Helms at the Dry Goods Shop and Mr. Potter at the Lending Library—the most eligible bachelor in the county.

Nora thought it preposterous that people considered the words wealthy and eligible to be synonymous. Why was everyone convinced that money and lineage made a person more desirable? Did character count for nothing? Nora had seen enough of Mr. Rutherford's behavior to know that the man had nothing to offer that would tempt her. His wealth, tall build, light blue eyes, and distinguished jawline might be enough to attract equally uninteresting women seeking a handsome face or security in his wealth and position, but such things would never matter to Nora. She valued integrity and honor above all.

Lulabelle sprang up, jumping on Major, and the large dog fell over and laid on his back, acting as if she had bested him.

Nora rolled her eyes, though she could not hold back a smile. "Stop acting the flirt, Major."

"Aren't they delightful together?" Mrs. Shaw said. "Though they are such an oddly matched pair."

"They are," Nora agreed. "However, I'm afraid Lulabelle's master would not agree on that point." She sighed. "I imagine I shall have to take her home."

"Durham Manor is on the other side of town." Mrs. Shaw's breath was labored as they started up the hill. "A journey of nearly three miles. Surely, Mr. Rutherford will come for his dog."

The memory of Mr. Rutherford's earlier accusations made Nora anxious to get the dog home where her master could not complain against her further. It wouldn't matter to him that Lulabelle's escapes resulted from his lack of care. Surely a man from such a renowned dog breeding family should know enough to not give an untrained dog complete freedom to roam.

"Perhaps we could find someone to deliver her," Mrs. Shaw said, breaking into Nora's thoughts.

"I'm afraid I must not allow any time to waste," Nora said. "But, the day is pleasant for walking, and with any luck, Mr. Rutherford will be away from home."

* * *

AN HOUR LATER, Nora came to the stone pillars that led to the grounds of Durham Manor. "Wait here, Major," she said, patting Major's head. She didn't think Mr. Rutherford would be pleased to see the dog again.

Major obediently plopped down in the shade, panting in the heat. He gave one small whine, looking at the dog in Nora's arms. She crouched down and let Major give his friend a farewell nuzzle, then walked between the pillars and followed the long drive leading to the Manor House. She had carried Lulabelle the last mile of the journey, and while the little dog was not heavy, she was warm, and combined with the summer sun, Nora was hot and perspiring, her clothes and hair sticking to her skin.

Nearing the house, she hesitated, wondering whether to approach the main doors, or should she find a servant's entrance? The dog's kennels were most likely behind the house, and she debated searching there for the kennel master.

The decision was made for her when the front doors opened and Mr. Rutherford himself hurried down the steps followed by a man in a tweed waistcoat and tall boots.

Seeing Nora and the dog, the men's shoulders relaxed visibly. Mr. Rutherford waved, and the pair changed direction, coming toward her.

Lulabelle lifted her head at the sound of their steps on the gravel.

"Miss Winters, you've found her once again." He inclined his head to Nora and gave the dog a gentle pat. "What am I to do with you, Lulabelle?" He spoke to the animal in a voice that was surprisingly gentle.

"I'm sorry, sir," the man in the waistcoat said. "I raised the kennel latch well out of her reach. Dunno how she managed to open it."

Mr. Rutherford gave the dog an affectionate look. "We'll just have to be cleverer than the hound, Mr. Babbage." He motioned toward Lulabelle. "Take her. Give her water and shade. And see to it that she doesn't escape again."

"Yes, sir." Mr. Babbage lifted Lulabelle from Nora's arms, pulled on the brim of his hat in acknowledgement, and started off toward the side of the house.

Nora brushed the wrinkles from her bodice, feeling heat in her cheeks. The last time she'd seen this man, she'd insulted both him and his dog and slammed the kitchen door. She saw now that she'd made some incorrect assumptions about how seriously Mr. Rutherford took his responsibility toward his dogs.

"Miss Winters," Mr. Rutherford said. "It seems I am in your debt once more."

"You've an intelligent dog, sir." Nora said, dispelling the discomfort of his surprisingly polite tone by focusing the conversation on a safe topic.

"She is that," he agreed. "And I thank you for returning her." He glanced behind her as if only just now realizing there was no carriage. "Did you walk all this way?"

She almost laughed at his expectation that just anyone could take a carriage wherever they needed to go, but she held it in. He'd behaved himself so far, and she could do the same. "It is a pleasant day." Nora folded her arms across her front to hide the wrinkles. "And I enjoy walking." She ignored the bead of perspiration that ran down her cheek at just that moment.

"I'll send for a carriage to take you home," he said.

His tone was courteous, but not friendly, suggesting his politeness was due to good manners rather than generosity. "I thank you, sir. But it is not necessary. As I said, I do enjoy walking. It gives me time to think." Nora glanced toward the pillars at the entrance to the property. "And Major is with me."

Mr. Rutherford followed her gaze toward the end of his drive. "You will at least want to cool yourself before the return journey. And your dog will require water." He motioned for her to precede him up the stone steps to the grand doors.

"Sir, it is really not necessary..." Nora began. With the man behaving so graciously and the evidence proving her assumptions about him wrong, she couldn't hold on to her anger. Losing it tore down a wall inside of her, leaving her vulnerable—a sensation Nora avoided above all others.

"I insist." Mr. Rutherford gestured toward the entrance. "A glass of lemonade is hardly sufficient payment for what you've done for me. You must allow me at least that much."

A reprieve from the sun and a cool drink were tempting, and allowing Mr. Rutherford his hospitality would ease future interactions if Lulabelle managed to outfox her handlers again. Nora nodded and walked with him toward the entrance.

A large wisteria tree stood to one side of the stone steps, its branches spreading wide to display hanging clusters of lavender-colored blossoms that contrasted stunningly against the honey-colored stone. The sight brought Nora up short, and she paused, admiring it. "This tree is spectacular," she said.

Mr. Rutherford glanced at her. "My mother planted it—years ago, when she first came to Dunford Manor—well before I was born."

"The fragrance must be divine at night." Nora glanced upward. "I imagine she placed it in this spot to enjoy the aroma through an open window."

He looked fully at her, now. "That was her design, exactly." He pointed at the upper story windows. "Her bedchamber was just there...she has been deceased for nearly ten years." He added the last bit quickly, answering the question before it was asked.

"I'm sorry," Nora said automatically. She studied the tree for a moment longer before they continued up the steps and into a grand entry hall.

"If you'll excuse me," he said, "I will arrange for lemonade. And send a groom tend to Major." He started away, but stopped, turning back. "The dog won't...attack, will he?"

She shook her head. "Only if he believes me to be in danger. He will not harm your groom."

He nodded and left.

Nora found herself alone, staring at an enormous globe-light chandelier. Beneath it was a round table that held a vase of fresh flowers, some of which were not native to the area, and others which could not possibly endure the summer heat. Dunford Manor must have a hothouse. She walked slowly around the table, studying the arrangement, noting varieties she'd never seen before. On one side of the entry hall was a lovely parlour. As she continued her circuit, she glanced through an open door on the other side and stopped, staring at the library.

The sheer number of books was astounding, reaching up two stories with a walkway around the upper level. She thought even the Old Bristol Library on King Street would be hard pressed to compete. The room must take up most of the north side of the house. Groupings of comfortable looking chairs and sofas were arranged on thick carpets before an enormous carved fireplace, and glass display cases held historical relics and valuable tomes. Nora stepped inside, turning for the full effect. Her gaze moved over the spines, as she read title after title; some familiar and others unknown. Her fingers tingled, and she ached to touch them, to lose herself in a story or delve into a scientific study. All the learning this room held. It was impossible to fathom. A lump formed in her throat, an ache she was all too familiar with.

"Oh, there you are," Mr. Rutherford's voice startled her, and she spun around.

A maid was with him, holding a tray with two glasses of lemonade.

At the woman's offer, Nora took one, and Mr. Rutherford the other.

He motioned with the glass to the room around them. "Quite a sight, isn't it?"

Nora nodded and took a sip, not trusting her voice. She hadn't realized how thirsty she was until the cool liquid hit her throat, and she was tempted to drink the entire thing in a gulp.

"My grandfather was, as you can see, something of a scholar," Mr. Rutherford said. "My mother considered donating the books and converting the space into something more useable. A ballroom perhaps, but I—"

"You mustn't," Nora interrupted. The moment the words burst from her mouth, she felt foolish. "I mean, of course you should do as you please," she amended. "But it would be a pity to dismantle such a magnificent collection."

"I could never bring myself to do such a thing, I assure you. Furthermore, I've only managed to read perhaps a quarter of the books so far."

Nora took a long sip to hide her discomfort in the realization that she and Mr. Rutherford both held a passion for literature. She actually envied whoever he ended up marrying, and she pitied him for the unlikeliness that his future bride would value the library and its contents the same way he did.

Nora needed to leave before she accidentally revealed any of these humiliating thoughts and led him to mistake her admiration for his library for interest in him. She looked for somewhere to set down the glass. "I should go."

His gaze turned thoughtful as he took her glass and placed it on a table beside a reading lamp. "You will want to rest first. Please, sit."

No, she couldn't. He was different than when they first met. Polite and thoughtful. Almost charming. But it was an act—his good breeding on display. And if she stayed longer and had a conversation, she might begin to forget that.

She glanced at her dirty skirts and sweaty bodice and pictured what she must look like. Most likely dust had settled into the perspiration on her face, leaving streaks of mud. "I am far too sullied, sir."

"Nonsense," he said. The coolness of his earlier tone was gone, and his words sounded genuine. "You really should—"

"Thank you for the lemonade, and for tending to Major." She'd interrupted him twice now, but she was becoming very aware of how she must look standing in this glorious room—and how she must smell. She started to walk past him, but Mr. Rutherford moved to block her way. "It would be no imposition at all to arrange a suitable ride for you and Major."

As tempting as she found that offer, she preferred he be in her debt than the other way around. "No thank you. Walking—"

"Gives you time to think," he said, interrupting her this time.

"Thinking the mind's nature, sir." She said the words automatically.

Mr. Rutherford raised his brows, making her feel even more aware of how very much she didn't belong here. Embarrassment at her appearance combined with the familiar ache at the reminder of what she'd lost made her desperate to leave.

She started past him, then turned, giving a small curtsy. "Thank you again, Mr. Rutherford. With any luck, Lulabelle will stay in her pen, and we shall not have to meet again." She meant her words as a jest, but they sounded impolite when she said them.

Mr. Rutherford's brow creased, but his expression did not change. He inclined his head and offered no further argument.

A moment later, Nora hurried up the path to the large stone columns. She thanked a frightened looking stable boy for tending to her dog and started off toward Westwood without a backward glance. The long walk would give her emotions a chance to settle.

"Come along, Major," she said "We're going home."

CHAPTER 3

*A*lastair sat on the sofa in Madame Dupont's dress shop while Miss Brittany and Miss Mumford were happily discussing gowns with the dressmaker. He had proposed the shopping expedition after Mrs. Mumford had conveyed to him Miss Brittney's disappointment at his missing the garden party. But after two hours in the same shop, he was regretting the gesture. Alastair switched to a more comfortable position, crossing one leg over and letting his gaze travel around the cluttered room, wishing for something to distract him from the tedium. He did not think it possible to produce an interested expression over one more scrap of lace or another fashion plate.

He glanced to the man beside him. Rupert Mumford, apparently accustomed to such outings, had promptly fallen asleep. Although he had never considered Mr. Mumford particularly clever, seeing him resting comfortably back against the pillows, hands crossed over his belly, Alastair thought perhaps the man was wiser than he let on.

"Mr. Rutherford, will you just look at the pattern on this damask?" Mrs. Mumford motioned for him to join herself and Miss Brittany at the dressmaker's table. "I think this color would do very nicely with Annalise's complexion, don't you?"

Alastair moved his gaze between the piece of cloth and Miss Brittany, trying to appear as if he were considering. "Very pretty."

Miss Brittany tipped her head to the side, looking up at him in a way that made her eyes appear larger.

The effect was charming, but it appeared forced. Alastair wondered if she had practiced the pose in a looking glass. He smiled, knowing it was expected.

"If you don't mind, ladies," Alastair said, once he'd estimated enough time had passed that he would not be perceived as rude. "I'll excuse myself for just a moment to visit the lending library." He glanced toward the door and then back to the piles of fabric and patterns. A book would make all of this waiting at least tolerable. And he wouldn't have to engage in the small talk that seemed to necessarily fill the silence.

"The lending library," Miss Brittany sniffed. "What a dull thing."

She and Mrs. Mumford exchanged a look that seemed to indicate they considered it an act of utmost patience to abide his eccentricities.

Alastair collected his hat from the hat stand next to the door and left the crowded shop. Though the day was quite warm, the breeze was welcome after the stuffy confines. He crossed High Street, continuing on in the direction of the small stone structure with tidy rows of books in its window. As he came near, he was surprised to see Major lying on the pavement beside the door. The animal's bulk made it impossible to pass him without stepping into the street. Alastair stopped.

Wherever Major was, Miss Winters was sure to be close by. Alastair considered turning back the way he'd come to avoid what would certainly be an uncomfortable reunion. When he'd last seen her a week ago, the young woman had walked three miles to bring Lulabelle home and insisted on walking the three miles back, suggesting a kindness behind her biting words and glances. In spite of her previous rudeness and unkempt appearance, he'd taken care to treat her with all the respect and hospitality he would show to any guests. While he genuinely wanted to express his appreciation to her, he had to admit that his politeness had been equally motivated by his certainty that

Lulabelle would eventually break out of her kennel again and put him in the same position.

Yet he'd been unexpectedly intrigued by Miss Winters, especially the way her face changed when she'd seen his library. It had reminded him of what a treasure his grandfather's collection was, a validation he sorely needed after the rest of his family dismissed the library as a waste of ideal socializing space and implored him to clear out the tomes in favor of something their friends would find more impressive.

So, he'd been unexpectedly sorry to see her go and confused at her abrupt exit. He had felt a door slam somewhere within her by the changes in her posture and a sudden desperation to flee from his presence. At first, he'd been offended and tried to dismiss it as another sign of her unconventionally, but dwelling on her behavior only made him more curious to unravel the mystery of Miss Nora Winters.

Unfortunately, he hadn't yet figured out how to go about this, and he'd certainly bungle any attempt now.

As Alastair debated whether he could suffer returning to the dress shop without a book, Major glanced up. Seeing Alastair, he sat straight, watching him with a gaze that appeared to be taking his measure. If Alastair backed away, Major would believe him submissive, and Alastair couldn't allow that. He would have to enter the library and show this dog who held the power.

"Good afternoon, Major," Alastair said, stepping around him and reaching for the door handle. The door swung open just as his fingers made contact. He pulled it wide to allow the patron to exit and saw Miss Winters pushing her way through doorway holding a basket on her elbow and an armful of books.

She looked up to see who had come to her aid. Her eyes widened, no doubt in surprise. "Mr. Rutherford."

Alastair tipped his hat. "Miss Winters."

She inclined her head. "Good afternoon, sir." She stepped outside, and the books shifted in her arms.

Alastair let the door close behind her and caught the topmost book as it fell, taking the opportunity to glance at the title. "The Critique of Pure Reason." He looked up at her, surprised. "You read Kant?"

She took the book from him and put it back atop the others, tucking them into the curve of her elbow.

"Is that so surprising?"

Alastair looked at the spines of the other books. "And Hume. My goodness, Miss Winters, are you a philosopher?"

She seemed to consider before she answered, studying him as if to discern whether his question was genuine. "I enjoy ideas," she said. Her voice sounded defensive. "And I am curious about why people behave as they do."

He nodded as aspects of their earlier interactions came into clearer understanding. Her interest in his library, the careful way she laid out her arguments concerning an animal's value. She had even quoted Descartes. All the more evidence that Miss Winters was not the contrary woman she portrayed, but one seeking truth and knowledge. Either way, she was a far cry from the women he usually interacted with who were more concerned with the pattern of their damask than attempting to understand human motivations.

"I didn't realize you are a scholar, Miss."

She watched him again, like a wild animal assessing whether he posed a threat, and as he heard his words again in his mind, he understood that she was weighing whether he'd just insulted her by dismissing her academic pursuits or mocking them.

"I'm sorry," he said. "I meant it as a compliment. Anyone reading these works is surely a scholar."

Her shoulders relaxed, and the suspicion faded from her eyes. "I would not call myself such." She glanced down at the books in her arms. "I am simply a reader."

"Scholars are nothing if not readers. Bear with me; it's been ages since I've engaged in anything more than gossip, small talk, or practical conversations. Your choice here indicates an inquiry into whether Kant's Categorical Imperative or Hume's Moral Philosophy has the greater merit. Have you reached a verdict? Or perhaps your reading has not yet covered the topics?"

"I'm familiar with the philosophies," she said.

"And your thoughts? Which do you prefer?"

"I see merit in both," she said, a brightness coming into her eyes. "But on their own, neither seems to be entirely complete." She motioned to the books with her chin. "Hence my need for further study."

She hefted the basket, shifting it back into the crook of her elbow.

"Shall we sit?" Alastair motioned toward a low stone wall not far from where they stood. "I would very much like to hear your opinions."

Miss Winters blinked. She glanced at the wall, and then back to him, looking utterly taken aback by his invitation. "Were you not going inside?" She turned her chin toward the lending library behind her.

"I'm surrounded by books all day," he said. "I'd much rather discuss human will and moral worth with a fellow scholar. You are not in a hurry, are you?"

The corner of her mouth pulled, and Alastair realized it was the first indication of a smile he'd seen on the young woman. Something inside him was very pleased by the sight, and he considered what might be required to entice the expression fully to fruition. "I have some time, and sitting sounds nice."

Alastair lifted the basket from her elbow, surprised by its weight. He glanced at its contents as they walked to the wall and saw wrapped parcels from the dry goods store as well as some bottles he assumed were from the apothecary. Surely the burden would make her return journey difficult.

The pair came to a spot in the shade and sat. Miss Winters stacked the books next to her, and Major hopped over the wall to sit on the cool lawn behind them.

Miss Winters surprised him by starting the discussion right away. "Do you believe humans have a moral obligation to duty, Mr. Rutherford? Or are we as a species purely motivated by sentiment?"

The question was a common one, especially among scholars of the two philosophers. And he had heard endless versions of the debate throughout his years at school. Alastair nodded, as if collecting his thoughts, but his answer was clear. In this he had no doubt. "An ethical person's choice is governed by duty, following a set of correct principles, no matter his desires or natural inclinations to do otherwise." It was a fact. Duty above all. It was the code by which Alastair had been raised. The tenet which directed his life.

"You make no allowance for individual circumstances?" Miss Winters asked. Her eyes seemed to sharpen into an intense gaze, and he could almost see her mind working.

"There is no exception," Alastair said. "Fulfillment of one's duty is the highest principle."

"No matter the consequence of one's action?" Miss Winters asked. A line had formed beneath her brows. She was thinking intently, listening to his words, considering them.

"That is correct," he said.

"You take Kant's position, then," she said. "The categorical imperative. If the intention is in line with one's duty, the result of an action is inconsequential."

"When it comes to a person's character, yes."

She tipped her head to the side and chewed on her lip as her brows drew tighter. It was a presentation she had obviously *not* practiced in the mirror, but in Alastair's opinion, its unstudied nature was what made it charming. A warm sensation grew in his belly, catching him so off guard that he almost missed her next question.

"And do emotions play no part in one's choices?" she asked. "For example, might a person be motivated to help another because of the happiness he will derive from performing a good deed? Or by the thanks he will receive?"

"One should never be ruled by sentiments," Alastair said. "Law, duty, and obligation." He remembered how often his father had repeated those very words. "Those must be the only factors in a person's decision." It had served him well thus far.

"But should one never perform an action simply to increase another's happiness?"

"If duty calls—"

"Oh, there you are!" Miss Brittany's words cut off his sentence. The young woman stood directly in front of him, one hand on her hip, the other holding a parasol. Mr. and Mrs. Mumford were nowhere to be seen.

Alastair rose to his feet. How had he not noticed her approach?

"You said you were going to the lending library." Miss Brittany looked at Miss Winters, and then back at him.

"I apologize," he said. "I came upon an acquaintance of mine." He motioned toward the young woman on the wall. "Miss Nora Winters, may I introduce Miss Annalise Brittany."

"How do you do?" Miss Winters said.

Miss Brittany nodded. "A pleasure." She let her glance travel over Miss Winters, and apparently seeing no reason to continue speaking with her, sniffed and turned back to Alastair.

Her behavior was rude, but it was hardly unexpected. Miss Winters and Miss Brittany moved in very different social circles; he was well aware. But seeing it gave him an uncomfortable feeling and an inclination to apologize, and not just for Miss Brittany. He'd acted in the same manner when she'd invited him into her home to reunite him with Lulabelle. Witnessing such treatment from this perspective flushed his cheeks warm with shame.

"Mr. Rutherford, if you don't mind, we must continue on," Miss Brittany said. "The Mumfords await us at the tea shop. We have yet to visit the milliner." She held up one finger and then another, listing off the tasks still to be done, Miss Winters long forgotten. "And Mr. Mumford is eager to see the haberdasher's new shipm— Oh Gracious!" Miss Brittany screamed.

Major had risen up from behind Miss Winters, putting his forepaws onto the wall for a better view. On his hind legs, he stood taller than Miss Brittany, and possibly even Alastair.

Miss Brittany jumped back, dropping her parasol and tripping over her skirts.

Alastair lunged forward and caught her elbow, saving her from a fall, but unfortunately, he was unable to prevent injury to her pride.

He would have to thank Major later for interrupting her tedious chatter.

Once she'd regained her balance, Miss Brittany clung on to Alastair's elbow. She looked between him and the dog. "What is that...that monster? It's hideous." Her voice was high pitched and loud. "Mr. Rutherford, you must do something."

"Down, Major," Miss Winters said calmly.

The dog dropped back so only his head showed above the wall.

"I'm sorry my dog frightened you, Miss Brittany," Miss Winters said, not looking sorry at all. "He's simply curious."

"That animal is a menace," Miss Brittany said, her voice a shriek. "You saw how it threatened me, didn't you, Mr. Rutherford?"

"Major is hardly threatening once you grow accustomed to his size." Alastair picked up the parasol and brushed it off before handing it back to her. "Shall we join the Mumfords for tea?"

"I intend to speak to the town council," she said. "A dangerous animal should not be allowed to roam free."

"Come along," Alastair said. "I assure you there is no reason to fear a dog just because it startled you." He took Miss Brittany's arm and turned toward the tea room.

When he turned back to bid Miss Winters farewell, the young lady was hurrying away in the other direction, the basket back on her elbow and her stack of books balanced on her hip. Major loped along beside her.

The uneasy feeling returned and stayed for the remainder of the day. Alastair resented the superficial conversations as the others discussed society scandals and the latest fashions, His thoughts were constantly pulled back to Miss Winters. He regretted she'd had to manage the heavy basket on the journey home, and he wondered what was she thinking of as she walked. And what was her opinion on Kant and Hume's classic debate? They had been interrupted before he had the chance to find out.

CHAPTER 4

a knock at the door startled Nora from her reading. She marked her page with a ribbon and closed her book, exchanging a surprised glance with Mrs. Shaw. Since moving to the new house, they had only been visited by the vicar and his wife. Mr. Rutherford might be a third visitor, but she hardly thought of his uninvited intrusion as a visit.

Mrs. Shaw set aside her knitting and sat up straight on the sofa, and both women tilted their heads toward the doorway, listening. Perhaps one of the new acquaintances they had made at church was now calling on them.

They heard the door open and the muffled sound of the part-time housekeeper, Mrs. Harris speaking to the visitor. A man's voice spoke in reply, and Nora supposed it must be the vicar, as their church acquaintances had all been women.

A moment later, Mrs. Harris came through the parlour doorway. "Mr. Rutherford to see you, Miss Winters." The housekeeper did not attempt to hide her curiosity as she announced the man's visit. She stepped aside, allowing him to enter.

Nora drew in a quick breath as her thoughts flew back to their encounter in town. Miss Brittany must have spoken to the mayor, and

Mr. Rutherford had arrived to deliver a complaint against Major. She could not imagine another reason for the man to pay a call. How else could she explain the nervous way he clutched his hat in his hands and stumbled for an appropriate greeting?

Mr. Rutherford swallowed and gave a slight bow. "Good afternoon, Miss Winters." He nodded toward Mrs. Shaw.

"Good afternoon, sir." Nora gestured to her friend on the sofa. "I don't believe you've met Mrs. Shaw. She is my dear friend since I was a child." She motioned back toward him. "And as to my relationship to Mr. Rutherford, I'm still sorting out what exactly it is."

She'd meant to imply that she didn't know if he bore bad news, but she had sounded coyly flirtatious. Surprisingly, this didn't bother her.

He inclined his head, a glint in his eye revealing he'd caught the unintended message. "A pleasure."

Mrs. Shaw did not rise. She smiled, showing dimples in her round cheeks. "How do you do, sir?"

Mr. Rutherford's manner didn't seem to imply he bore the weight of a sentence against Major, but Nora needed to be sure. "We're delighted to have a visitor, but we weren't expecting you. What brings you here?"

"I am very sorry to bother you ladies by arriving unannounced," Mr. Rutherford said. "But it's Lulabelle. She's run off again, and I wondered if she may have returned here?"

The relief Nora felt was incomplete. She may not need to worry about Miss Brittany's complaints today, but she did have to worry about Lulabelle's safety and whether Mr. Rutherford intended to voice his displeasure about the low-class company his most precious dam insisted on keeping.

"Such a mischievous pup," Mrs. Shaw chuckled. "Keeps you on your toes, doesn't she, sir?"

Nora braced herself for a comprehensive lecture on the great importance of Mr. Rutherford's breeding hound and her value to the huntsmen of the British Empire.

But his response could not have been further from her expectation. Mr. Rutherford chuckled in return.

Nora stared at the man, stunned by the change in his visage. His smile brightened his eyes and lifted his cheeks, making furrows like parentheses on either side of his mouth. She wondered if Miss Brittany had kissed that mouth, and the jealousy that arose inside her took Nora by surprise.

Nora's chest went hot, and her stomach hitched, then flopped over. She looked away, horrified at her unbidden response, and even more horrified that someone may have seen it. She refused to entertain any notion of laying claim to Mr. Rutherford's affections. His duty demanded he marry someone like Miss Brittany, and he'd said himself that he held duty above all else, no matter the personal cost. She'd been silly to assume they'd engaged in a flirtation earlier.

Mr. Rutherford shook his head at Mrs. Shaw's observation, still chuckling. "She indeed keeps me on my toes, Mrs. Shaw. The little imp foils all of our efforts to contain her." Mr. Rutherford shook his head and laughed. "The kennel master believes she climbed onto the roof of the shelter in her pen, reached her paw between the slats in the gate to unfasten the latch, then jumped back down to make her escape."

Mrs. Shaw laughed along with him, holding her hand to her side. "The naughty thing."

Nora fought against the blush stealing up her neck and determined to focus the conversation on the matter at hand. "I'm afraid I haven't seen Lulabelle, Mr. Rutherford. But if she's nearby, Major will have intercepted her."

"Miss Winters, might I persuade you to accompany me to inquire with Major?" Mr. Rutherford asked.

The blush threatened again, but Nora held it at bay. Mr. Rutherford had not come to seek out her company. He was here for his dog and undoubtedly apprehensive about approaching Major alone.

Nora nodded.

Mrs. Harris, who had not moved from the moment she entered the parlour snapped into action. She hurried down the passageway ahead of them, and when they reached the door, she handed Nora her hat and a shawl.

Nora, her mind a jumble, took the hat, fastening it with a pin, and pulled the shawl around her shoulders.

Mr. Rutherford, still holding his hat, placed it on his head as they stepped outside. Several steps from the house, Nora realized the weather was far too warm for outerwear and pulled the shawl off her shoulders, draping it over her arm.

"The housekeeper only comes a few days a week." Nora spoke to dispel the silence as the pair walked down the hill toward the stream. "On those days, Major stays outside. He tends to keep sentry on this path through the woods." She glanced at Mr. Rutherford and instantly regretted it, as he was looking intently at her.

Nora snapped her eyes back in the direction of the path and called out, "Major!"

A sequence of low barks answered her call, and a higher pitched bark joined in. Mr. Rutherford sighed loudly, either in relief or in resignation. "Lulabelle."

They hurried toward the sound, stepping easily across the terrain that had given poor Mrs. Shaw such trouble. Nora walked several miles each day out of necessity and had the strength to prove it, but she doubted Mr. Rutherford chose to walk when he could ride a mount or a carriage. His dexterity and surefootedness impressed her.

A moment later, the animals came into view, making their way toward their masters. The dogs were playing as they had before, chasing and frolicking. Major ran past with the smaller Lulabelle right behind. He slowed, letting her catch him, then turned and chased her in the other direction.

"I'm sorry, sir," Nora said, starting toward the dogs. "I'll fetch her."

"One moment, Miss Winters." He caught her arm, stopping her. He motioned to a shaded spot—the same place she'd proposed to Mrs. Shaw as suitable resting spot, giving a small tug on her arm. "The dogs are enjoying themselves. And if you don't mind, I should like to continue our discussion from the other day."

"Oh." Nora looked toward the trees, then at her arm where Mr. Rutherford still held her elbow.

"I'm so sorry," he said, realizing the familiarity of his grip and pulling his hand away. "Allow me to start again. Would you care to sit?"

Her cheeks warmed. "Yes, of course."

Mr. Rutherford offered his hand. "May I?"

She placed her hand in his, and he maneuvered it to rest onto his arm then led her to the shady spot beneath the beech tree. When they reached it, she pulled her shawl off of her arm and shook it straight to lay it on the ground. Mr. Rutherford took it from her and spread it out for her to sit on.

Nora could not gain hold of her thoughts. Her bewildering reactions to Mr. Rutherford made her feel as if she were not in control of her own emotions. That they persisted in spite of her knowledge that he would always be duty bound to marry someone of his station further frustrated her. She sat, adjusting her skirts, taking a calming breath, and reminding herself that they were simply here to supervise their pets and have an interesting conversation while they were at it.

Mr. Rutherford sat beside her. He stretched out his legs, crossing them at the ankle and leaned back onto his hands. He looked at her expectantly. "And so, Miss Winters, you have heard my argument. Now, it's your turn. Tell me, is the heart of morality defined by duty or sentiment?"

"I do not believe the matter is that simple, sir," she said. "I see both virtues as essential principals of an ethical person."

"Indeed?" he raised his brows and motioned with a tip of his head that she should continue.

Nora studied his expression, looking for any indication that he was mocking, but seeing none, her confidence bolstered, and she continued. "If man was simply meant to obediently follow laws, why was he given emotion at all? To make the performance of his duty more difficult? To give him impulses that are simply to be overcome? I don't believe that to be the case." She picked up a twig, poking it into the ground as she spoke. "The feeling of unease or surety as a decision is made should not be ignored. An action does not become less virtuous because it was dictated by intuition instead of obligation."

She stopped speaking, watching as the dogs made their way to the edge of the river to drink.

Mr. Rutherford tensed, his eyes following the animals. Nora knew Major wouldn't allow Lulabelle to come to any harm, but Mr. Rutherford had disengaged from their conversation. She called Major away from the river to ease her companion's concerns.

As she expected, Lulabelle followed, and Mr. Rutherford turned back to her. "Your argument, then, is that emotions can be considered sufficient motivation, even at the expense of one's understood duty. I prefer to follow duty and obligation because the rules are something we can agree upon as a community. Meanwhile, emotions vary greatly from person to person."

"That's true," Nora said. "But I believe a person must learn to trust his own conscience. There are times when it is nobler to act on sentiment than duty. And there are times when the rules society dictates are wrong or harmful, even contradictory."

"Such as?"

Nora paused to collect her thoughts, and she appreciated that Mr. Rutherford busied himself watching Lulabelle to allow her the time she needed. After a few moments, she said, "Society has agreed that lying is wrong, meaning we are duty bound to tell only the truth. Yet there are times when speaking the truth can cause pain. Society also agrees that we should not cause pain. To uphold one duty, I must deny the other. So long as the lie won't cause harm, my conscience tells me to prioritize my duty to spare others from unnecessary pain, so I choose to lie."

Major lopped over to lay in the shade between them, and Lulabelle followed, lying beside him.

"You consider a falsehood to be more virtuous than the truth?" Mr. Rutherford asked.

Nora stroked the dog's thick fur as she considered. She had been extremely bold in her opinions, especially knowing they were so removed from Mr. Rutherford's own beliefs. But the informality of their relationship as well as their circumstance gave her courage.

It wasn't as though he were a potential suitor whose feelings she needed to coddle, anyhow. His social position was so far above her own, she felt no worry about consequences should he take offense. He would simply cease speaking with her

She was unaccustomed to this sense of freedom, and she reveled in how comfortable it felt. It gave her the confidence to speak her mind freely, something she'd not done with anyone, aside from Mrs. Shaw, in years.

She nodded. "I suppose I do find virtue in a falsehood in some cases."

He scratched Lulabelle's head, and the dog closed her eyes.

The poor pup was quite worn out.

"Such as...?" he prompted

"Such as telling a child you enjoyed her performance on the violin when it was, in truth, quite dreadful."

Mr. Rutherford chuckled, and both dogs looked up at him, irritated that their rest had been disturbed.

"In this case," Nora continued, "the truth might prove harmful to the child's confidence, and she may choose never to pick up a bow again." She rested her hand on Major's side. "Or what of telling a lady how lovely she looks in her new gown, when she in fact..." She let her words trail off, allowing Mr. Rutherford to finish the thought.

"Ah, yes." He grinned. "We all know better than to make that mistake. But as you mentioned, polite behavior may be considered a matter of duty and therefore..." He held up a finger, as if the discussion were over and his case had been made. "...either of these examples illustrate perfectly Kant's Categorical Imperative. Duty over all."

"You've misrepresented my meaning. When we began this conversation in town, I argued that both philosophies held merit, but that they were incomplete. Kant does not sufficiently account for when duties contradict one another, and Hume tends to overlook the role duty plays in our perception of moral behavior. When I combine the two perspectives, I note circumstances when duty becomes confused. At these times, we must beseech our consciences to weigh the consequences and make the final choice, making emotion the highest authority without discounting duty entirely."

Mr. Rutherford nodded and sat up straighter, leaning toward her. The intensity in his blue eyes made her glad they were seated. She was not sure her legs would have supported her as he eagerly watched for her reaction as he spoke. "While you display impressive logic, if duty lays the foundation for conscience, as you say, that makes morality and our consciences dependent upon duty. Thus, duty is the highest authority."

Nora opened her mouth to argue, but seeing his teasing grin, she smiled in return. He turned and reclined back on his elbows again and gazed over the river, sinking deep into thought and releasing her from whatever magic he'd cast. She enjoyed the silence for a few minutes as her heartbeat calmed, thinking on the points he'd made.

She liked that they could sit comfortably in their own thoughts rather than filling the empty space with whatever came to mind. Nora found small talk exhausting, but this conversation, extended silences and all, invigorated her.

"You pointed out the conflict that can arise between obligations," Mr. Rutherford said, putting his weight on one elbow and turning to face her. He didn't meet her eyes this time, instead running his hand thoughtfully over the grass. "I must admit that you've made me consider things from a different perspective, as I can't deny your point that duty does become confused. But there are also times when morality is equally confused and duty must drive the decision. In a few minutes of thought, I identified several examples throughout history when we've amended our morality based on greater under-standings."

"For instance?" Nora asked.

"The English translation of the Bible comes to mind. The Church, arguably the greatest moral authority of the time, consid-ered the translation so blasphemous that William Tyndale fled England to go into hiding. He was eventually martyred because his duty to expose and prevent corruption outweighed a flawed moral-ity. Yet today, that morality has changed. We do not argue over whether Tyndale selected the correct English word or whether churchgoers should be able to read and interpret scripture for themselves. If anything, we take that opportunity for granted and praise his poetic language."

Nora saw a clear path of debate and struck immediately. "I would say that Tyndale's duty was to support church authority, and his conscience drove him to work in opposition to that duty."

Mr. Rutherford flopped onto his back and covered his face with his hands. Nora quickly identified the shaking of his body as laughter.

"You are wonderful, Miss Winters," he said finally, wiping his hands down his cheeks to dry his eyes. "I do not admit defeat, though I will be constructing my counterargument for days."

Nora's face warmed at the compliment, and she joined her laughter with his. "You do make an excellent point, and I'm sure it will also keep me distracted for days."

"We're destined to argue in circles forever, aren't we?"

The word *forever* struck Nora and forced her to look away. Surely he meant nothing by it.

"Shall we agree, then to disagree?" Nora struck up her courage and looked at him again.

"If you like." He shrugged a shoulder, his expression becoming more serious. "But I confess, I do enjoy the discussion. May I reserve the right to reopen it again?"

Nora couldn't fight her smile at the thought of a future conversation. She hoped it would not require an act of fate or a tenacious dog to instigate it. "I would enjoy that."

Mr. Rutherford held out his hand for her to shake, and she took it, pretending it meant nothing when she really felt the heat of his palm race up her arm and warm her whole chest.

"Though I'm not quite ready to go home," he said, releasing her hand. "Am I keeping you from your . . ." His face turned red. "I assure you, I'm not attempting to reignite the debate so soon when I ask if I'm keeping you from your *duties.*"

Nora laughed. "I do prefer to stay out of the housekeeper's way when she's working. But as we're abandoning Misters Kant and Hume, how shall we pass the time?"

He studied her with a glint in his eye, and she glimpsed the mischievous boy and the rowdy youth that still existed within this man who now carried the weight of his family estate on his shoulders.

"How shall we pass the time?" he repeated, and Nora's throat tightened at the realization of how flirtatious she'd sounded.

And was he flirting back? She forced herself to take measured breaths, unwilling to give him any indication of the effect he had on her.

Mr. Rutherford didn't linger on the question. "You told me you are not a scholar, but you have been educated, certainly. Where did you attend school?"

Nora followed his lead and shifted her weight to sit on one hip, her legs tucked to one side. "Picton Ladies' Academy in Bristol. But I only attended for a short time."

"And why is that? You certainly have the mind to continue on to University."

She frowned, looking toward the river. "My family had neither the funds, nor the opinion that a woman should be educated." She sighed as the familiar ache tightened her stomach. "Mrs. Shaw sponsored me at the academy, but when her husband died and her children took over management of her funds, they...didn't think it a worthwhile investment."

Mr. Rutherford remained silent, watching as she spoke. She couldn't tell from his expression what his opinion was on the matter, or even whether he had one. "Mrs. Shaw took a bad fall, soon after. Fractured her femur, and her recovery was extensive. The family thought I would be better suited as a companion, especially after the amount of assets that had already been invested in me. Truthfully, I would have cared for her out of friendship, but few people believe as much, considering my position as companion provides for me where I cannot provide for myself."

Her face was hot with shame at the admission of her need for charity and the humiliation of having it rescinded, but she thought it necessary to emphasize the difference in their stations. If Mr. Rutherford had been flirting with her, it could come to no good end for either of them. While she intended to discourage thoughts he might be entertaining of making advances, she found it liberating to speak of her circumstances to someone who had no part in the situation.

"I was surprised to learn Mrs. Shaw was a friend." Mr. Rutherford said. "I had assumed she was a grandmother or aged aunt. How did you come to know her?"

"When I was seven, I invaded her library while she and her husband were out for the day." She gave a sheepish smile. "Although I have no memory of the incident. She 'took me under her wing,' you might say, encouraging my curiosity and providing opportunities for learning. The Shaws had no children of their own, you see, and she was happy for a child to dote on. And I believe my parents were happy for one less to worry about."

She scratched Major, smiling at him when he opened his sleepy eyes to look up at her. "It is because of Mrs. Shaw that we have Major."

Mr. Rutherford turned his body to face her directly, almost mirroring her position, though he chose a more masculine posture, sitting first cross-legged and then raising one knee to rest his elbow upon it. He glanced down at the dog. "I've wondered about Major's origins since making his acquaintance."

"He was just a puppy when I discovered him, half-starved in an alleyway between my parents' house and the Shaw's." She let her fingers run over his thick fur. "I just couldn't leave him, but I also couldn't take him home where we had no space or food to spare. Mrs. Shaw allowed me to keep him in a shed at her house, but once he'd outgrown the little enclosure, she was quite attached." She smiled, patting the dog. "I learned from her servants that she would sneak bits of sausage to him when she thought nobody was looking. No wonder he is so loyal to her."

Major looked up at her again, somehow knowing they were talking about him.

"He is loyal to both of you," Mr. Rutherford stood, brushing off his trousers and holding out his hand. "If only I could instill that level of obedience in my own hounds."

Nora took his hand, allowing him to help her stand.

He picked up the shawl, shaking it out before giving it to her. "I am sorry that our outing must come to an end," he said, lifting Lulabelle into his arms. "But, I'm afraid I've an obligation this evening."

They shared a knowing smile to acknowledge the word they were supposed to be avoiding in their agreement to disagree.

He chuckled softly and glanced up to where clouds were forming in the western sky.

Nora hadn't noticed. Nor had she realized how much time had passed. The sun indicated it was early afternoon. They must have been visiting for hours.

Major led the way back to the house, and the party walked in silence. A niggle of doubt worked its way into Nora's thoughts. Had she let her growing attraction show and unintentionally encouraged him? Why else would he possibly wish to know about her childhood? She could only hope he'd listened politely as a gentlemanly obligation, a matter of duty. The bit of doubt grew until it was heavy in her belly. He hadn't merely listened; he'd asked her to share.

When they reached the kitchen door, Mr. Rutherford inclined his head. "Thank you for a very pleasant visit, Miss Winters."

Determined to dissuade him, she said, "I fear I talked too much, sir. I suppose when my social circle consists of Mrs. Shaw, the house-keeper, the vicar, and his wife, I am overly eager to converse with someone closer to my age who is kind enough to listen. I apologize for presuming a man of your station held an interest in my humble story."

His voice was sincere and low. "Please don't apologize. I enjoyed our conversation very much. If either of us was over eager, it was me. It is not often that I am afforded the opportunity of a thoughtful discussion." He glanced down at Lulabelle and toward where his horse waited. "I fear my opportunities for such will soon decline."

"Sir?" Something about his tone worried her. He sounded resigned and...wistful. Her mind fell on the only answer that made sense. He had already or would soon tie himself to Miss Brittany or some other woman like her. Nora ached for him. Marrying Miss Brittany out of duty meant he'd have precious few, if any, chances to be the delightful man she'd just spent hours conversing with.

And she would most likely never have the opportunity to see that man again.

"Sir," she asked again. His teasing and smiles were entirely absent, and a heaviness settled on his shoulders.

Nora was all but certain he was confronting the same unpleasant reality. She wanted to curse Kant and his obsession with duty. When two people got along like she and Mr. Rutherford had, why should society's ideas of proper duty interfere?

A curtain moved aside in a nearby window. Mrs. Shaw peered out and immediately retreated, letting the curtain drop. The brief distraction was enough to pull Nora and Mr. Rutherford from their heavy thoughts.

"It seems I'm the one who must apologize," Mr. Rutherford said. He offered no further explanation. Lulabelle danced on her hind legs at his feet, seeking his attention. Mr. Rutherford gave a deep sigh as he picked her up, but not even his beloved dog could lessen the pain on his face.

Nora wanted to comfort him with a hand on his broad shoulder, but she didn't reach out. The action was too familiar, and it wasn't her place. She knew there would be more behind the gesture than friendly assurance. It would only lead to her getting hurt.

She took a step back, suddenly eager for him to be on his way so she could gain control over her emotions and give herself a stern lecture. "Whatever is troubling you, I'm certain it will be well." She spoke formally, placing even more distance between them through her tone.

He let out a heavy sigh. "It must be."

CHAPTER 5

*A*lastair watched in the mirror as Renn knotted his ascot. He hadn't even attempted to do it himself. His mind was distracted, covered with a gloom that he could not shake. He glanced toward the window, noting the rain that had begun as he rode home from Miss Winters's home was continuing steadily.

"Are you well, sir?" Of course the valet had noticed Alastair's malaise.

"I am." Alastair spoke forcefully in an attempt to convince them both. He put his arms into his coat and blinked a few times to rid himself of the doldrums.

"If you say so, sir." The pinch at the edges of the valet's eyes indicated his lack of conviction.

Miss Brittany and the Mumfords were due to arrive, and Alastair needed to present the cheerful front akin to a bright, sunny day, regardless of the dark storms of discontent within him. So far, he couldn't even muster the somber cheer of a light spring shower.

"A fine knot, Renn," Alastair said, studying his presentation in the mirror. His waistcoat was new, as fitted the occasion.

The sound of a carriage on the drive drew both their gazes to the window. Alastair sighed. He bid Renn good evening and started down the stairs. Duty above all, he reminded himself. An alliance with Miss Annalise Brittany is what his father would have wanted. It would be advantageous for the estate as well as his family line.

A voice came into his thoughts. A voice he'd tried all day to ignore. *"There are times when it is nobler to act on sentiment than on duty."*

Alastair sighed again, motioning for the footman to open the doors to the dark drizzle that mirrored his current sentiment. "Unfortunately, Miss Winters," he muttered beneath his breath. "This is not one of those times." The melancholy returned, heavy and cold, but he mustered his will, shoving it away.

He remained in the doorway as the footman started out into the rain with an umbrella, meeting the carriage as the driver opened the door. Mr. Mumford stepped out and opened his own umbrella, holding it over his head as he assisted both his wife and Miss Brittany from the carriage.

The ladies took shelter beneath the footman's umbrella, linking arms and looking up at the Manor House as they approached.

"Didn't I tell you?" Mrs. Mumford's voice carried in spite of the pattering of rain. "The house is unmatched in beauty. It's a pity the clouds are so heavy. When the sun shines on the golden stones, it practically glows. And I've heard the plumbing's been updated."

Miss Brittany bent to look up beneath the edge of the umbrella. "That tree is dreadful," she said. "Right beside the main entrance? It throws off the symmetry and ruins the entire effect. And those roses...so old fashioned, aren't they?"

Alastair's jaw tightened. But his mother's insistence on proper social manners overrode his instinctive reaction. He bowed when the ladies came up the steps. "Welcome, Mrs. Mumford, Miss Brittany."

The ladies stepped through the doorway, paying their respects. Mr. Mumford followed behind, and the men exchanged greetings as a maid took away wet hats and cloaks. The three glanced around the entryway, the Mumfords having visited the Durham estate only once before, to attend a hunting party years earlier. He didn't believe they'd ever been inside the Manor House. Since his mother's death, Alastair and his father had hosted very few social events. And because of the renovation, this was the first time he'd entertained since his father's funeral.

"I'm very delighted that you accepted my invitation," Alastair said to the three gathered in his entry hall. "In spite of the weather."

"The rain is refreshing," Mr. Mumford said, hooking his thumbs in his waistcoat pockets. "First time in months that I haven't been overheated."

"The weather certainly takes away any opportunity of seeing your fine grounds," Miss Brittany said. "I've heard your gardens are the most exquisite in the county."

Alastair recalled her comment about his mother's roses and forced a smile in spite of it.

"A tour of the grounds will have to wait for another day," he agreed. "But, as we have some time before dinner is served, perhaps you would care to see the house?" He offered his arm to Miss Brittany, and when she took it, he led the group through the various sitting rooms, the portrait hall, and the conservatory.

As Alastair told snippets of his family's history and interesting facts about the building, he watched Miss Brittany's reaction, trying to imagine her as mistress of the house.

She seemed, for the most part, interested, but something about the calculated way she studied the rooms gave the impression that she was considering how she might change them. It was perfectly natural for a young woman to wish to make a house her own, and he had no objection to updating the décor that had remained virtually the same for ten years. But her mental planning itched at him, and it didn't go away.

The group came, at last, to the library. As it was the house's most dramatic feature, Alastair was not surprised by the exclamations and awe from his guests. Mr. Mumford, in particular, expressed his wonderment. "My father described this room to me, years ago. But his words did not do it justice in the least."

Mrs. Mumford stood before the enormous hearth, studying the carvings on the mantel. "Such craftsmanship," she said, reaching to touch a carved leaf.

Alastair turned to the young lady at his side. "Would you care to see an original King James Bible from 1611?" He motioned toward a glass case beneath the window. "It is the pride of my grandfather's collection."

"I confess, I find books to be very dull." She sniffed, giving the same dismissive expression as she'd given Miss Winters in Westwood. The memory brought with it a burst of anger that surprised Alastair, both at how Miss Brittany had treated his friend and how Miss Winters refused to leave his thoughts. She would see this Bible for the treasure it was, and judging from their conversation by the river, would know a good deal about its historical value.

It was no matter. Alastair knew his duty.

He glanced toward the decanter of brandy on a side table, thinking he really should have had a drink before his guests arrived. His apprehension about this evening and what it meant for his future had brought about unexpected emotions. He needed to calm himself.

He blamed Miss Winters for his current predicament. He'd been happier before he knew she existed, content in the path laid before him by his parents and generations before. He would have accepted courting Miss Brittany as the natural order of things. Now he wanted to question everything, but he couldn't allow himself the luxury.

"Mr. Rutherford," Jameson, the butler, spoke from the library doorway. "Dinner is ready, sir."

Alastair thanked him and led his guests to the dining room. He sat at the head of the table with Miss Brittany at his right and the Mumfords on his left. The first course was served, and he dipped his spoon into the soup, glad for something warm on the dreary day.

"Delicious," Mrs. Mumford said, as she took another spoonful. "I do hope your cook will share the recipe."

"I'm sure that can be arranged." Alastair said.

A crack of thunder made them all glance up at the ceiling.

Alastair turned to the young lady on his other side. "Miss Brittany, how are your parents? When we last spoke, you mentioned your mother had been unwell."

"Yes." Miss Brittany set down her spoon and dabbed her lips with

45

the corner of her napkin. Her table manners were impeccable. "She's had a dreadful time of it, the poor dear. And her coughing has kept the entire household awake."

"That must be so difficult." Mrs. Mumford's voice was filled with sympathy.

"It is," Miss Brittany agreed. "You know how I need my sleep." She sighed, motioning to a footman with a flick of her fingers for her soup bowl to be removed. "I simply cannot manage if I don't have a full night's rest. And it has become frustrating to speak with her in between her fits of coughing that I've stayed away from her sickbed all together."

Alastair took another spoonful of soup. He could not think of any response to such a comment, but as the host, he knew he needed to keep the conversation flowing. Besides, deepening his acquaintance with Miss Brittany was the objective of the dinner party. "And your father?" he asked. "Is he in good health?"

"Quite good health," she said as a footman laid another plate before her. "He spends nearly every day off on some hunt or another. I rather think he is avoiding the coughing as well, to tell the truth. It does grate on one's nerves."

"That puts me in mind," Mrs. Mumford said. "Had you heard..."

Servants bustled around the table replacing empty soup bowls, serving the next course, and refilling glasses. As he watched to ensure his guests' needs were met, Alastair lost track of the conversation. His thoughts drifted to those horrible days when his mother lay on her sickbed.

He or his father had remained constantly at her side, reading to her or simply holding her hand as she'd coughed and coughed while consumption ravaged her lungs. The memory of holding a kerchief to her mouth when she'd become too weak to do so, only to take it away spattered with blood was so vivid that his chest ached.

The very idea of leaving her alone in her illness was so appalling that he considered whether it would be appropriate to pay a call on Mrs. Brittany's mother, just so she would have company.

Without warning, Miss Winters intruded upon his musings. She would be equally abhorred by the situation. She'd taken on the care of Mrs. Shaw when her friend's family determined the lady too much of a nuisance.

"Don't you think so, Mr. Rutherford?" Miss Brittany's voice pulled him from his contemplation.

"I beg your pardon," he said, cutting into his pork and hoping his face didn't betray the guilt he felt over dwelling upon the virtues of a woman he could never court. "What was the question?"

"Mr. Dobson's hairpiece!" Mrs. Mumford declared. Both of the women snickered. And Even Mr. Mumford chuckled. "You must have noticed it at church."

"I admit, I hadn't—" Alastair began, but he didn't have the chance to finish his sentence before Miss Brittany spoke.

"Why does the man insist upon such a poorly made toupee?" She tapped the top of her head and the others laughed again. "Does he think nobody will notice? Marianne Parks claims she saw a gust of wind nearly take it from his—" A chorus of barking sounded from outside, cutting off the young lady's words and drawing her eyes toward the window. "Oh dear, what is that racket?"

"Feeding time," Alastair said, smiling as he imagined the dogs jumping up in their pens, unable to wait patiently for their meals to be distributed. "The hounds get excited for their food."

"What a terrible din." Miss Brittany set her napkin onto the table. She looked toward the window again, her lips pressed together. "Well, at least the beasts are not allowed inside the house.

She could not have been more wrong, but Alastair chose to remain silent. Some of the mature hounds remained inside during the cold months, warming their old bones at the hearth. And if a dam or her litter needed extra care, the library became a temporary whelping shed or, as Mr. Babbage joked, a 'puppy hospital.'

When the meal was finished, he motioned for the footman to clear their plates and rose to his feet. "I'd hoped to speak to Miss Brittany alone for a moment before the ladies withdraw. If you don't mind, miss."

Miss Brittany shared a glance with her friend and looked up at him, making her eyes large as she'd done before. "Of course, sir." A footman pulled back the young lady's chair and she stood, taking Alastair's arm.

Alastair had considered this part of the evening carefully. His original intention had been to take her to the gardens, but the rain ruined that plan before her disdain for roses had a chance to. He'd next thought to take her to the library, but seeing her earlier reaction, he thought better of it and led her to the parlour beside the entryway instead. It was as good a place as any, he concluded. And she wouldn't be able to hear the dogs.

At his invitation, Miss Brittany sat on a sofa, and he took a seat facing her. Even though it was raining, the window was slightly open, letting in the aroma of his mother's wisteria. Miss Winters had immediately inferred why it had occupied that space, and Miss Britany had merely scoffed at it as dreadful.

Alastair took a breath, bracing himself.

"The feeling of unease or surety as a decision is made should not be ignored." Miss Winters's words came into his thoughts, but he shoved them back out, determined to push through and have it done.

"Miss Brittany," he began.

"Yes, sir?"

Her eyes were enormous, her lower lip extended in a pout. She was extremely lovely, and yet, Alastair felt only dread as he looked at her. It seemed as if his heartbeat had even become sluggish. He cleared his throat, wishing he could clear his mind as well. "In the weeks since making your acquaintance, I have become quite…"

Alastair swallowed, as if doing so might un-stick the words from his throat.

"Yes, Mr. Rutherford?" Her pout intensified and she tipped her head to the side.

"I have become…What I mean to say is, you and I…I'd hoped…" His thoughts would simply not fall into line

She smiled sweetly. "What are you saying, sir?"

"I wish to ask you, miss, if you held any objection to—"

A pounding on the front door stopped his words, and he jumped to his feet.

The relief at the interruption made his limbs weak with relief. He opened the parlour door to investigate and could not resist this taste of freedom. The air inside had become heavy and stifling.

"Mr. Rutherford?" Miss Brittany spoke behind him, rising to her feet.

"Please excuse me," he said. "Something must be amiss."

He arrived at the front door just as Jameson pulled it open, revealing a very wet, very upset Nora Winters. In spite of her appearance and her obvious distress, Alastair's heartbeat quickened.

Miss Winters's gaze moved past the butler, and when it landed on Alastair, she wiped her cheeks, whether to rid them of tears or rain, he couldn't be sure. "Mr. Rutherford." Her voice cracked in a sob. "It's Major. I've searched for hours, and...he's simply gone."

CHAPTER 6

*N*ora stood on Mr. Rutherford's doorstep feeling utterly humiliated as tears ran down her cheeks. She only now realized how pathetic she must appear, weeping, muddy, and soaked through.

Mr. Rutherford pushed past the butler, coming into the rain and taking her hand. "Miss Winters, you'll take ill. Come inside immediately and warm yourself."

A footman brought an umbrella, holding it over the pair of them.

"There isn't time, sir," Nora protested, even as Mr. Rutherford pulled her out of the rain and into his entry hall. "Something is wrong. I'm certain of it."

A woman—Miss Brittany, Nora remembered—stepped into the entryway from the parlour. "What is this?" Her expression could not have been more disgusted if a pile of mud had plopped into the entryway.

"I am so sorry to interrupt." Nora looked down at the puddle growing beneath her boots. She felt even more foolish than before, knowing Mr. Rutherford had a guest. She should have gone straight to the kennels to ask after Major, but remembering how he'd come to her directly earlier, she'd thought to pay the same courtesy. Now she regretted it.

A maid brought a towel, and Mr. Rutherford took it, putting it around Nora's shoulders. "Now, tell me what's happened." His voice was low and gentle.

"Major stays outdoors when the housekeeper comes, as I told you." Nora said. "But he remains close enough to hear when I call. He's always come. Always."

"And he did not today," Mr. Rutherford guessed.

Miss Brittany puffed out a noise of displeasure.

A commotion sounded from deeper in the house, and a moment later, Mr. Babbage came into the hall, every bit as wet and muddy as Nora.

"What impertinence," Miss Brittany said. "Surely a servant knows better than to cause such an uproar."

Mr. Rutherford ignored her. "Mr. Babbage, what is it?"

The kennel master looked as if he were going to be ill. "Sir, I don't know how it happened again. Truly, I locked the pen and double checked that it was fast, but once feedin' time came…"

"Lulabelle." Mr. Rutherford's voice was not as calm as it had been a moment earlier.

"Yes, sir. I—" Mr. Babbage looked miserable.

"Prepare my buggy," Mr. Rutherford said.

The kennel master hurried away as Mr. Rutherford continued giving orders.

At his words, the servants rushed into action. Nora couldn't believe the swiftness with which he managed the situation. She just hoped they weren't already too late.

"But what about our dinner party?" Miss Brittany looked furious.

Nora shrunk back, feeling the woman's ire directed at her.

"I beg your pardon, miss." Mr. Rutherford removed his dinner coat and put on a tarapaulin jacket brought by a maid. "Please make my apologies to the others."

"Is this about your dogs?" Miss Brittany motioned at the activity around her to indicated what she meant by "this."

51

"It is," Mr. Rutherford said, panic edging his words. "I'm afraid it can't be helped." He turned to Nora. "They're most likely together, and if Major isn't coming when called, something is very wrong."

A maid removed Nora's wet coat and helped her into a raincoat similar to Mr. Rutherford's.

"Sir, I will not be so easily dismissed," Miss Brittany raised her chin, glaring at both Mr. Rutherford and Nora. "Especially for such a person as this."

"Good evening, Miss Brittany." Mr. Rutherford tipped his hat before motioning for Nora to precede him out the door.

Moments later, the pair hurried up the dark road in a two-person cabriolet. Blankets and towels sat at their feet and over their legs. Although the buggy's roof covered their heads, Nora still held an umbrella against the rain that blew or dripped inside. As miserable as she was, she took comfort in Mr. Rutherford's steady presence. He'd been preparing to leap into action to help Major even before he'd learned of Lulabelle's latest disappearance.

Mr. Rutherford managed the reins, squinting ahead into the darkness and urging the horse onward toward the town.

"Where are we going?" Nora asked. She'd gotten into the buggy simply trusting that Mr. Rutherford would know what to do and allowed herself to be lulled into a sense of security just being with him.

"Each time Lulabelle has gone missing, we've found her at the same place—near the river. I have no reason to believe she'd change her pattern, now. At the very least, we start there and work our way back toward the manor. Once you showed Major the way to my estate, he might have paid Lulabelle a call."

A sick feeling settled in Nora's heart. "The river was so deep, and moving fast." She clutched tightly to the umbrella handle. "Something bad has happened. I know it." Tears returned, stinging her eyes. "Mr. Rutherford, I fear Major has come to harm. And possibly Lulabelle as well."

He tensed, and in the darkness, she could see his frown was grim.

"We'll find them, Miss Winters. Major is as intelligent of an animal as I've ever seen."

"Lulabelle is impressive, as well."

"That she is." Mr. Rutherford shook his head. "Cecil Babbage has tended my family's kennels for over twenty years. I know the man to be diligent and careful. He's never lost a dog before. Not one accident. But in the last two weeks..." He sighed. "Lulabelle. That hound has given him more trouble than he deserves."

Nora appreciated his attempt to calm her with conversation. "I am so sorry about this, sir. I didn't mean to interrupt your evening."

He glanced at her from the side of his eye, but kept his concentration on driving. "You were right to come to me."

"But your guest," she protested. "If I'd known..."

"Do not spare it another thought," he said. "In truth, I was glad to see you."

"I can't imagine that was the case," Nora said.

"Miss Winters, do you accuse me of telling a falsehood?" He shook his head as if he were disappointed. "After our discussion this morning, you know I abhor such a practice."

"Unless manners dictate it," she reminded him. "You are trying to spare my feelings."

He glanced at her again, the shine of his eyes gleaming for a moment in the darkness. "I tell you, I don't lie. For example, a liar would tell you that you did not look like a drowned rat at my front door this evening." His lips twitched, but he kept his gaze on the road. "I make no such claim."

In spite of her worry, Nora chuckled. She still did not think he was pleased to see her wet and muddy on his porch in the middle of his dinner party, but his words set her at ease. At least he wasn't angry.

The horse's hooves clacked on the paving stones as they rode through the town. Streetlights and houselights shone through the rain, but the reprieve from the darkness was short lived as they continued on, past Westwood.

At her direction, Mr. Rutherford drove the buggy to the little barn, leaving the horse inside, out of the rain.

They started down the hill toward the river, and Mr. Rutherford took her hand, walking fast. Nora carried the umbrella, but couldn't hold it over both of their heads, and it was more of an encumbrance when they were moving quickly, so she closed it and left it beneath the beech tree.

She called for Major, but heard nothing in return aside from the sound of rushing water and the rain.

Mr. Rutherford called Lulabelle's name and they continued on until they were directly beside the river.

"Have care." Nora raised her voice to be heard above the water and rain. "The mud is thick along the edge." She looked in both directions. "Should we separate?"

"No." He took her hand again. "It's safer to remain together."

Nora hoped the dogs had the same instinct to keep each other safe. She called for Major.

Alastair kept hold of her hand as they started downriver at a quick pace.

The rain had either slowed, or she'd become accustomed to the noise. Nora strained her ears and squinted, searching beneath trees and briars—anywhere the dogs might have taken shelter. She heard something in the distance, but feared she may have manufactured the noise from her imagination. She slowed, trying to still the sound of her breathing.

Mr. Rutherford turned back.

"I thought I heard something," Nora said. She called for Major, and this time there was no mistaking the answering bark.

Mr. Rutherford heard it as well. He pulled her forward, and the two ran toward the sound.

"We're coming, Major!" Nora recognized the cry for help. As she feared, something was wrong.

The barking grew louder as they approached the stone bridge. Major was atop it, in the very center of the river. Seeing him brought a wave of relieved tears to Nora's eyes. "Major!"

The dog ran to the edge of the bridge, then returned to the center, his distressed barking telling them to follow. He put his paws up onto the side of the bridge, his barks quick and loud.

"Where is Lulabelle?" Mr. Rutherford asked, his voice heavy with worry.

"There!" Nora pointed.

The little dog was beneath the bridge. She stood, balancing on a narrow ledge on the stones of the bridge's center piling, just above the waterline. Seeing them, she let out a flurry of panicked yelps. They needed to reach her before she fell or decided to make a jump.

Nora and Mr. Rutherford rushed onto the bridge, looking over the edge of the low wall. Lulabelle was far too low to reach.

Nora put her hand on Major's head. "Good dog," she said in a quiet voice.

"She must have been swept down the river. Thank goodness she was able to reach higher ground." Mr. Rutherford peeled off his coat and put his foot up onto the wall, ready to jump over. The water moved, fast and dark beneath them.

Nora grabbed onto his arm. "Wait."

He looked back, but the tension in his body indicated he had no intention of waiting.

It's too shallow to jump," she said, surprised that he didn't seem very knowledgeable about the river after having lived herby. "You'll have to start from the shore, but once you reach Lulabelle, it will be dangerous to swim back while holding her. The safest way is up, and I'm not strong enough pull you out. But you can lift me."

He hesitated but shook his head. "No."

"Can you think of a better plan?" Nora asked.

He frowned, looking over the wall and then back to her. "The water moves faster than you think." It was as close to agreement as she could expect.

"I am a good swimmer and have become familiar with this river." She pulled off her own coat. "The water is only waist deep at most."

She ran off the bridge and up the riverbank, thinking she had a better chance of directing herself at the piling if she rode with the current instead of trying to fight against it.

She crouched down and untied her boots, leaving them in the mud at the river's edge. She'd never swam in her skirts before and thought better of trying it now. They would only catch the current and drag her along. She didn't look at Mr. Rutherford as she slipped out of everything below her waist besides her foundation garments, but she was certain she'd scandalized the poor man. She waded into the cold water, grateful for the temporary coverage it offered and cringing at the thought of Mr. Rutherford pulling her onto the bridge in such a state.

Almost immediately, the rush of water tugged at her, and as she went deeper, it pulled harder until her legs were swept out from beneath her. The water drew her downriver, and she kicked, fighting to get to the middle of the river so she could reach the piling before being swept beneath the bridge.

She came to the bridge faster than she'd anticipated, and nearly missed the piling, but she caught ahold of its edge.

She pulled herself around the piling so the water pushed against her, holding her in place. There was nowhere for her feet to gain purchase, so she clutched to the ledge, its roughness digging into her fingers. "I'm here, Lulabelle," she said, panting as she looked up at the little dog on the ledge a few inches above her.

Lulabelle whined. And although she was frightened, Nora could see the bridge had offered some protection from the rain. At least the poor animal was dry.

"Nora?" Mr. Rutherford called from above. "Are you down there? Nora?" Hearing her Christian name gave her a start. She looked up, seeing his shadow overhead.

Major was beside him. He barked once.

"I'm here," she called back. "Lulabelle appears to be unharmed." Nora used the stones of the piling to pull herself up a few inches to where she could reach the frightened animal. "Do not fear, Lulabelle," she said in a gentle voice. She reached to scratch behind the dog's ears.

Lulabelle whined again. She was shaking.

Nora drew herself a bit higher. But it was more difficult than she'd expected. The river wanted to push her past the piling, and her arms and legs ached with the exertion of holding herself up and fighting the current. "I can't raise myself out of the water. Do you have anything I can tie to Lulabelle's collar?"

"Catch onto this!" Mr. Rutherford called. Nora felt something brush across the top of her head. She caught one end of his suspenders. He held the other tight.

Nora attached the suspenders to Lulabelle's collar, calling up when it was secure.

The dog yelped as she was pulled off her feet, and continued yelping as she dangled over the river. Nora hoped the collar would hold and the little dog wouldn't slip out.

After a few anxious seconds, Major gave a bark of approval, and Nora knew Lulabelle was safe.

"I've got her," Mr. Rutherford yelled. He lowered down the suspenders again. "Now you! Put the collar around your wrist!"

Nora was tempted to sink back into the water, just to let her muscles rest. Her limbs trembled with the exertion of holding herself up. She used the last bits of her strength to grab on to the woolen strap and saw that Mr. Rutherford had pulled Lulabelle's collar through a buttonhole, creating a loop. She pushed her right hand through the collar and gripped the strap hard with both hands as she was lifted up and out of the river. Once free of the current, she swung in the opposite direction.

Mr. Rutherford's hand clasped on her left one, then his other was on her wrist, and she hung, dangling by her one arm over the water, the suspenders swinging from her right wrist.

Her wet skin slipped lower in his grip, and he grunted, exertion plain on his face.

Nora screamed as she imagined falling and being swept downriver.

"Take my arm, Nora." Mr. Rutherford didn't yell. His voice was commanding; a man used to giving orders and having them obeyed.

She did as he asked, but her grip had already exhausted itself. If he jerked even the slightest bit, she'd lose her hold.

In one motion, he shifted one hand from her left wrist to her right, his grip painfully tight. In a second motion, he heaved, pulling her up and over the wall. Nora's bodice and bare legs scraped over the stones and she fell, landing on top of Mr. Rutherford, who'd rolled backward and used his body to cushion her.

Major barked, rushing to her. Mr. Rutherford lifted her to sit and wrapped her into a tight embrace, trying to rub warmth back into her arms.. He grabbed her coat and wrapped it around her shoulders. "What was I thinking, allowing you to do that?" He turned his attention to her hands and wrists, freeing her wrist from the collar and rubbing at the red mark it left. "Never again, Nora. Do you understand? You could have fallen. I should never have allowed it."

She'd never seen him so flustered. He spoke in circles as he embraced her. "Mr. Rutherford," she said softly into his ear. "Mr. Rutherford."

"What if you had fallen? Or been swept away downriver?"

"Alastair!" She said his name firmly and he pulled away, his hands on her arms as he looked at her face. He raised one hand to brush her hair aside and rested it on her cheek.

And then he kissed her.

Warmth spread through Nora, melting away the cold and fear. She should have been outraged that he'd taken such a liberty, but it felt exactly right. Was he capable of reconsidering his familial obligations? She softened with hope, one hand touching his chest. His body was hot, in spite of the rain, and Nora could feel his heart beating under her fingers.

The kiss lasted only an instant. Mr. Rutherford pulled back. Jerking away as if he'd been stung. "I beg your pardon. I—" He pulled back further. "I should not have done that."

Nora's ribs squeezed tight, and she swallowed hard. Of course. He'd been swept up in the heightened emotions and forgotten his important obligations. The kiss had been an action of relief, brought on by the heat of the moment. Nora's eyes and cheeks burned as she reached for Major, and humiliation roiled in her belly, made worse by how foolish she looked with barely a coat to cover her.

What had she been thinking? Now that the excitement had cleared, she wondered if she had made the decision to endanger herself based on duty or emotion. Perhaps it didn't matter, so long as she made the decision that she would not regret. She would never have abandoned Lulabelle.

Mr. Rutherford retrieved her clothing. Nora refused his offer to help her dress and ungracefully supported her balance by leaning on Major as she stumbled into her skirt and shoes. Mr. Rutherford turned his back to give her privacy. He held Lulabelle in his arms, and the dog watched her struggle from over his shoulder. How could such a tiny creature create so much havoc in her life?

CHAPTER 7

*A*lastair tugged on Lulabelle's lead, directing her to walk beside him instead of pulling ahead. He sighed. If only the hound didn't run away every day, they might have made progress with her training. How Lulabelle managed to have such energy after the harrowing events of the night before was anyone's guess. As for himself, Alastair was exhausted. By the time he and Lulabelle had arrived home and were dried and warm, the hour was nearly dawn.

The lead jerked in his hand. Lulabelle must have ascertained their destination. Alastair had purposely walked the longer route through town, both to avoid the river as well as to give himself time to think. Miss Winters was right in that regard. A long walk was the perfect opportunity to examine one's thoughts, and he had many thoughts demanding examination.

Last night, everything had shifted. Or, rather, last night, he'd fully admitted to himself a truth he'd known all along. That he had fallen in love with Miss Nora Winters.

Admitting it had produced a peace he'd not felt for years. A calm that was so opposite of the unsettled state Miss Brittany produced in him that it made him reconsider his entire assumption that sentiments were simply obstacles to the performance of one's duty.

He'd trusted his intuition when it came to searching for Lulabelle last night. He'd trusted it over the years in choosing the best breeding hound from a litter, hiring an estate steward, and when he'd decided to attend Oxford rather than his father's school, Cambridge. And so why was he so opposed to following it when it came to a question of marriage?

The realization had changed everything, clearing away his conflicting thoughts and leaving him confident and surprisingly hopeful. A smile pulled at his mouth and he lifted his face, letting the sun warm his skin. Hopeful, indeed.

They came within view of the house, and Lulabelle let out a bark, pulling again on the lead.

Major came around the side of the house, and Alastair released his hold, letting the animals race off together. He followed them, discovering Miss Winters among lines of hanging laundry—blankets and towels from the night before. His heart jumped, further confirming his decision.

Miss Winters looked up, and seeing Alastair, her cheeks colored, and she turned to her task of hanging another towel.

Mrs. Shaw sat on a chair in the shade, laughing at the antics of the dogs.

Alastair tipped his hat to the older woman and stepped between the rows of laundry toward Miss Winters. "Good morning."

"Good morning, Mr. Rutherford." She nodded but made a decided effort not to look at him, and instead lifted a wet blanket from a basin and laid it over the line.

Alastair pulled an end of the blanket, straightening it. "I thought Lulabelle might enjoy calling on her friend."

Miss Winters looked at where the dogs were chasing one another around a tree.

Alastair watched the unevenly matched pair. His earlier defenses when it came to his prize dam's association with the mixed-breed had reversed completely. He'd not have admitted it earlier, but Lulabelle had been perceptive in her choosing of Major as a friend, in spite of his questionable pedigree. The dog had proven himself a loyal protector.

"Major certainly appreciates the visit," Miss Winters said. She clipped a pin onto a corner of the blanket to hold it in place. "Thank you."

"Miss," he offered his arm. "Might I speak with you?"

She glanced at Mrs. Shaw, then at his arm, and finally lifted her gaze to his. She held herself tightly as if she were braced against what he might say. "If this is about..." Her face flushed again. "You've no need to explain, or to apologize. I hold no resentment. I've put the entire incident from my mind completely."

"I'm afraid I haven't. In fact, I've thought of nothing else." Seeing that she wasn't going to walk with him, he turned to face her directly. "Miss Winters, last night changed everything." He closed his eyes and swallowed as the memory resurfaced. His grip slipping, the terror, like cold bands compressing his chest. "If you'd fallen..." He cleared his throat. "That moment was a revelation. I knew, then—although, perhaps I'd known it since you showed up at my house carrying Lulabelle—that nothing mattered more to me than *you*."

"Sir?" she tipped her head to the side, as if unsure that she'd heard him correctly.

"I am in love with you, Nora Winters." In his earnestness, he spoke louder than he'd intended.

The two of them looked at Mrs. Shaw.

The older woman appeared to be watching the dogs, but the still way she held herself and her overly innocent expression indicated she was listening closely.

"Nora Winters," he lowered his voice so only she could hear. "Would you do me the very great honor of consenting to be my wife?"

Miss Winters took his arm and pulled him toward the river and away from the prying ears and eyes of Mrs. Shaw. "Are you telling me that your view has changed? That you side with Hume and the moral sense theorists above Kant's Categorical Imperative?"

Alastair barked out a laugh. "Do you intend to use my declaration of love as an opportunity to win a debate?"

She shook her head, confusion still furrowing her brow. "I simply meant...I assumed your intentions were inclined in a different direction. She grimaced but held his gaze. You must realize I have nothing to offer, that our union would benefit you, neither monetarily or socially. Surely, your duty to your family and your name would—"

Alastair touched his finger to her lips, stopping her words. "My intentions are inclined in your direction, Nora." He stepped closer, lifting her chin and sliding an arm around her waist. "And, I hope for the sake of my heart that yours are the same.

Nora studied his expression, and she must have concluded that he spoke in earnest, because her arms went around him, and she kissed him. The action took Alastair by surprise, but, he reasoned, the man marrying Nora Winters should accustom himself to being surprised.

Her lips were warm and soft, and she kissed him with a certainty that was exhilarating. Alastair tightened his arms, holding her close against him as their lips moved together. He kissed her cheek, her chin, her neck, eliciting a small gasp that spiked through his nerves like electricity.

"You've given me no answer," he teased, whispering the words against her skin.

Nora drew back. One brow lifted and her lips pressed together as if she were suppressing a smile. "I imagined you to be a student of Aristotle's teachings on deductive reasoning. But perhaps I've not given you sufficient premises on which to base your conclusion." She tugged on his ascot, crumpling the pressed silk in her fist as she pulled him closer until his face was just inches from her own. "I will do so, now." She kissed him again, more boldly this time, expelling all thoughts of philosophers. There was only Nora, and in that moment, she was everything.

SADDLES & SCOUNDRELS SERIES

The Connecting Door

The Wolf of Heathclove Manor

Pride & Pedigree

BOOKS BY JENNIFER MOORE

The Sheik's Ruby

Always 'Twas You

Change of Heart

Safe Harbor

Becoming Lady Lockwood

Lady Emma's Campaign

Miss Burton Unmasks a Prince

Simply Anna

Lady Helen Finds Her Song

A Place for Miss Snow

Miss Whitaker Opens Her Heart

Miss Leslie's Secret

My Dearest Enemy

The Shipbuilder's Wife

Charlotte's Promise

Wrong Train to Paris

Solving Sophronia

Inventing Vivian

Healing Hazel

www.ingramcontent.com/pod-product-compliance
Lightning Source LLC
Chambersburg PA
CBHW070647130626
46555CB00006B/2750